Jasper's Beanstalk

Nick Butterworth and Mick Inkpen

Bradbury Press   New York

Maxwell Macmillan International
New York   Oxford   Singapore   Sydney

On Monday
Jasper found
a bean.

On Tuesday
he planted it.

On Wednesday
he watered it.

On Thursday
he dug and raked
and sprayed and
hoed it.

On Friday night he picked

up all the slugs and snails.

On Saturday he even mowed it!

On Sunday
Jasper waited
and waited
and waited…

When Monday came around again he dug it up.

"That bean
will never make
a beanstalk,"
said Jasper.

But a long   long

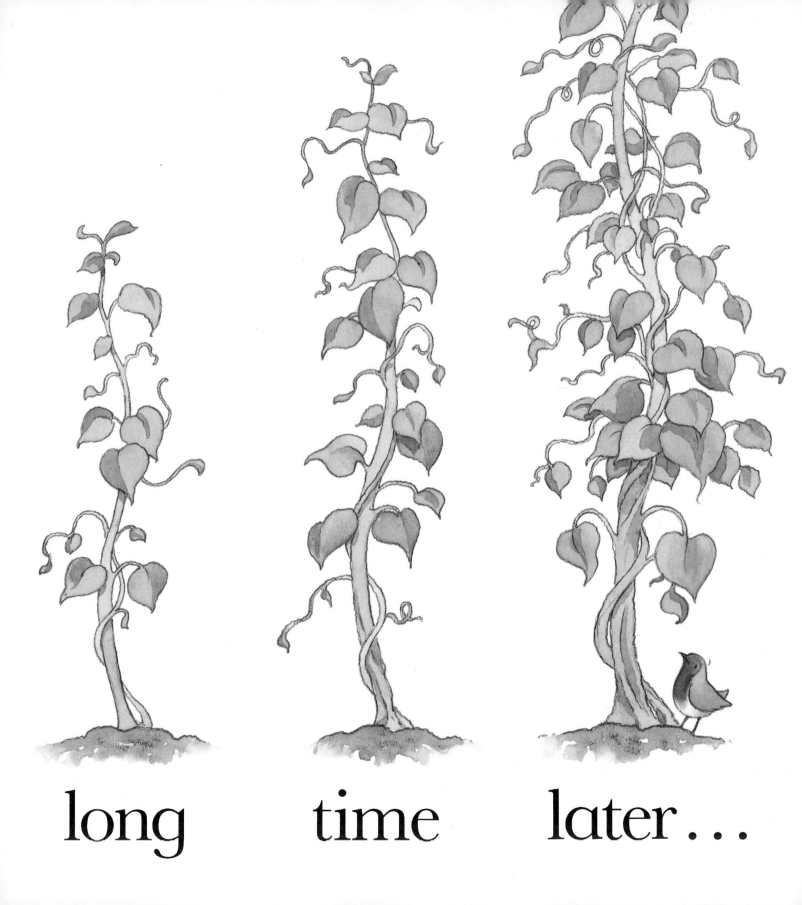

long   time   later . . .

It did!

(It was on a Thursday, I think.)

Now Jasper is looking for giants!

Library of Congress Cataloging-in-Publication Data   Butterworth, Nick.   Jasper's beanstalk / by Nick Butterworth and Mick Inkpen. — 1st American ed.   p.   cm.   Summary: Jasper hopes to grow a beanstalk, but becomes discouraged when the bean he plants doesn't grow after a week.   ISBN 0-02-716231-1 [1. Beans—Fiction. 2. Cats—Fiction.] I. Inkpen, Mick. II. Title. PZ7.B98225Jas 1993 [E]—dc20   92-14886